For Matilda, with love—H.W.

For Cain—W.A.

Text copyright © 2004 by Helen Ward

Illustrations copyright © 2004 by Wayne Anderson

All rights reserved.

CIP Data is available.

Published in the United States 2004 by Dutton Children's Books,

a division of Penguin Young Readers Group

345 Hudson Street, New York, New York 10014

www.penguin.com

Originally published as Twenty-five December Lane in Great Britain 2004 by Templar Publishing,

an imprint of The Templar Company plc, Surrey, Great Britain

Designed by Mike Jolley

Edited by A. J. Wood

Printed in Belgium          First American Edition

ISBN 0-525-47300-9

1  3  5  7  9  10  8  6  4  2

HELEN WARD

# Finding Christmas

Illustrated by WAYNE ANDERSON

Dutton Children's Books

NEW YORK

*It* had been a long and dreary
December. And here it was—Christmas Eve.
For weeks, the little girl in the red coat
had been searching for the perfect present
to give to someone very special.

Now night was falling, and time was growing short.

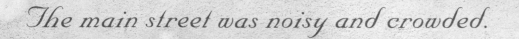
The main street was noisy and crowded.

The girl was stepped on . . .

pushed and jostled...

and squeezed off the busy
pavement...

. . . into the damp gloom of

## December Lane,

which was as gray and cold and empty

as a winter without Christmas.

❧

Any ordinary shopper would have turned back,

but the girl in the red coat wasn't

ready to give up. Maybe, she thought,

the perfect gift is just waiting to be found

here in this overlooked corner of town.

As she peered into the shabby windows,
her hope began to fade.

There was nothing special here—
only shops full of spare parts and old teapots
and dusty, dead insects. She shivered and pulled
her coat more tightly around her.

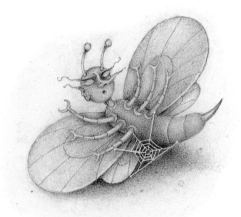

Just as she was about to turn back,
a glimmer from across the street caught her eye.

A patch of warm light spilled from a shop window
she couldn't recall having seen before.
It was heaped with toys and games, and the girl could
see that the shop was bustling with activity.
As she pushed open the door,
a bell on a spring rang merrily.

❧

# A little breath of Christmas

slipped past her, out into December Lane
and up to the dark gray clouds.

❧

She closed the door carefully behind her
and stood staring in wonder.

She had never seen
**so many toys!**
Surely she could find an
extra-special present here.

Teddy bears and model trains,
books and dolls and dinosaurs
were piled on high shelves and long countertops.

At one of the counters,
another customer was being helped.
Shop assistants raced around, crossing items
off a long shopping list.
"Excuse me," said the girl politely.
"I'd like to find a—"
"I'll be with you shortly," came the answer.

❧

Up and down the ladders the assistants flew.
The girl watched as one shelf
after another became empty.

"Can you help me?"
the girl asked a hurrying assistant.
"I see you have a—"

"Just a moment," he replied.

❧

The other customer, who barely fit
into his huge gray coat and well-worn hat,
scooped games from the shelves into his sack.
"Surely he's not going to buy
everything?"
But the passing assistant just
waved a dismissive hand.

❧

The other customer looked her way
as he bustled past.
From under the brim
of his hat, she thought
she caught the wink
of a kind and
twinkly eye.

The toys continued
to roll and scuttle into the enormous sack.
They rattled and pinged
and squeaked and whistled
until the floor, the counters,
and every shelf
were cleared...

...as if by magic.

The girl looked on in dismay.

Soon the other customer was ready to leave.

He tied his great sack shut, slung it over his back,
and somehow squeezed through the door,
leaving just enough space for a cheerful

"*Merry Christmas!*"

❧

"I'm very sorry, miss,
but we have nothing left to sell,"
said the chief assistant, turning to her at last.

The girl in the red coat felt her heart sink.
She would just have to continue her search elsewhere.
"Not to worry," whispered the assistant with a secret smile.
"Sometimes the best presents are the ones that find us."

The girl stepped outside and gazed up
into the darkness, swirling with snowflakes.
It had been a dreary December and a dismal
Christmas Eve, but the town in its fresh white coat
looked beautiful. The girl smiled at the thought
of how much the special someone waiting at home
would love this snow.
It wasn't something she had bought in a store,
but it was still a gift they could share.

As she turned toward home,

the girl heard the faint, merry ring of a bell.

She looked up, and something

tumbled toward her out of the sky.

With a flurry and a gentle thud,
a little breath of Christmas
landed at her feet.

❧

It was **exactly** what she
had been searching for!

An extra-special present . . .

*for an extra-special brother's*
*very **first** Christmas.*